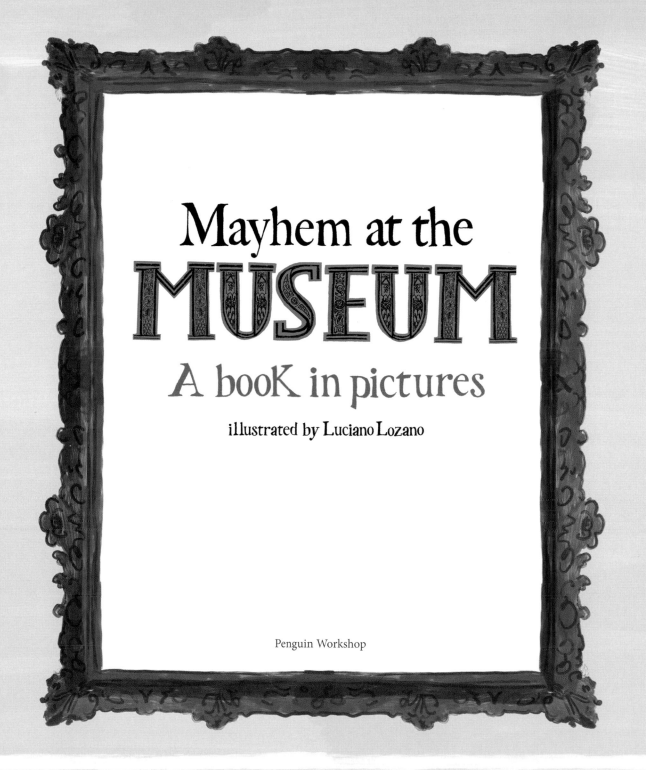

# Mayhem at the
# MUSEUM

## A booK in pictures

illustrated by Luciano Lozano

Penguin Workshop

**To Fernando—LL**

PENGUIN WORKSHOP
An Imprint of Penguin Random House LLC, New York

*Mr. and Mrs. I. N. Phelps Stokes* (John Singer Sargent): The Metropolitan Museum of Art, New York, Bequest of Edith Minturn Phelps Stokes (Mrs. I. N.), 1938;
*Two Young Girls at the Piano* (Auguste Renoir): The Metropolitan Museum of Art, Robert Lehman Collection, 1975;
*Self-Portrait with a Straw Hat* (obverse: *The Potato Peeler*) (Vincent van Gogh): The Metropolitan Museum of Art, Bequest of Miss Adelaide Milton de Groot (1876–1967), 1967;
helm for the Joust of Peace (*Stechhelm*): The Metropolitan Museum of Art, Bashford Dean Memorial Collection, Gift of Edward S. Harkness, 1929;
*A Woman Seated beside a Vase of Flowers (Madame Paul Valpinçon?)* (Edgar Degas), *Bouquet of Sunflowers* (Claude Monet), *Bridge over a Pond of Water Lilies* (Claude Monet),
and *The Little Fourteen-Year-Old Dancer* (Edgar Degas): The Metropolitan Museum of Art, H. O. Havemeyer Collection, Bequest of Mrs. H. O. Havemeyer, 1929;
*Merengue en Boca Chica* (Rafael Ferrer): The Metropolitan Museum of Art, Purchase, Anonymous Gift, 1984;
*Still Life with Apples and a Pot of Primroses* (Paul Cézanne): The Metropolitan Museum of Art, Bequest of Sam A. Lewisohn, 1951;
*At the Lapin Agile* (Pablo Picasso): The Metropolitan Museum of Art, The Walter H. and Leonore Annenberg Collection,
Gift of Walter H. and Leonore Annenberg, 1992, Bequest of Walter H. Annenberg, 2002;
*Young Woman with a Water Pitcher* (Johannes Vermeer): The Metropolitan Museum of Art, Marquand Collection, Gift of Henry G. Marquand, 1889;
*María Teresa (1638–1683), Infanta of Spain* (Velázquez [Diego Rodríguez de Silva y Velázquez]): The Metropolitan Museum of Art, The Jules Bache Collection, 1949

www.metmuseum.org

The publisher does not have any control over and does not assume any responsibility for author or third-party websites or their content.

Visit us online at www.penguinrandomhouse.com.

Library of Congress Cataloging-in-Publication Data is available upon request.

ISBN 9780593093542     10 9 8 7 6 5 4 3 2 1